What If Everybody Did That?

by
Ellen Javernick

illustrated by
Colleen M. Madden

two lions

two lions

Text copyright © 2010 by Ellen Javernick
Illustrations copyright © 2010 by Colleen M. Madden

Text first published in 1990 by Childrens Press, Inc.
Original text copyright © 1990 by Childrens Press, Inc.

Amazon Publishing
Attn: Amazon Children's Publishing
P.O. Box 400818
Las Vegas, NV 89140
www.amazon.com/amazonchildrenspublishing

Library of Congress Cataloging-in-Publication Data

Javernick, Ellen.
    What if everybody did that? / by Ellen Javernick;
illustrated by Colleen M. Madden. — 1st Marshall
Cavendish Pinwheel Books ed.
        p. cm.
    Summary: A child learns that there are consequences of
thoughtless behavior, from feeding popcorn to a bear at
the zoo to dropping an empty can out of a car window.
    ISBN 978-0-7614-5686-5
    [1. Behavior—Fiction.] I. Madden, Colleen M., ill. II. Title.
    PZ7.J329Whd 2010
    [E]—dc22   2009005938

The illustrations are rendered in mixed media.
Book design by Vera Soki
Editor: Nathalie Le Du

Printed in China

To Mike, Becky, Andy, Matt, Lisa,
and their families.
— E.J.

For my Peej, Sean, and Gabe,
who never leave handprints on a cake.
— C.M.M.

When we went to the zoo, I fed just a little of my popcorn to the bear. The zookeeper waved his broom and said, "What if everybody did that?"

I just wanted to see how fast the grocery cart would go. It went faster than I expected! When the manager stopped me, she said, "What if everybody did that?"

On the way to visit Grandma and Grandpa in Kansas, I dropped just one soda can out the window. The patrolman who pulled us over said, "What if everybody did that?"

At Uncle William's wedding, I took just a little lick of the frosting from the fancy cake. The lady behind the table glared at me over her glasses and said, "What if everybody did that?"

I told the babysitter that I took a bath just once a year. As she shooed me into the bathroom, she said, "What if everybody did that?"

During story time I had something important to say. I just couldn't wait till the end of the story. The librarian put her finger to her lips and said, "What if everybody did that?"

While we sat in the car waiting for Dad, I honked the horn.
I just honked a few times, but Mr. Thompson came to his door.
He shook his head and said, "What if everybody did that?"

At the swimming pool, I just splashed a little.
The lifeguard blew his whistle and said,
"What if everybody did that?"

On the bus, I just stood up to see the fire truck. Mr. Gearshift glared at me in the rearview mirror and said, "What if everybody did that?"

Just once I didn't hang my coat on the rack at school. Ms. Sanders made me pick it up and said, "What if everybody did that?"

At recess, I threw just one snowball at Sammy.
Mr. Walters saw me. When he sent me to stand
by the wall, he said, "What if everybody did that?"

When we went out for dinner, I just shot one straw wrapper. The waitress stopped taking our orders and looked straight at me. She said, "What if everybody did that?"

After the football game, I just ran on the field to get the quarterback's autograph. The official waved his arms and said, "What if everybody did that?"

When I came home I gave my mom a hug.
What if everybody did that?

Everybody should!